Marx Joyce
Abbott Hardy Machiavelli Montaigne Chesterton Cooper Emerson Austen
Defoe Melville Haggard Hugo
Christie Eliot Grimm
Stoker Carroll Molière
Wilde Maupassant Byron
Fitzgerald Einstein Engels Schiller
Garnett Smith
Goethe Hawthorne Kafka
Cotton Dostoyevsky Hall
Baum Kipling Doyle Willis
Leslie Dumas Henry Nietzsche
Flaubert Turgenev Balzac
Stockton Vatsyayana Crane
Burroughs Verne
Curtis Tocqueville Whitman Gogol Vinci
Homer Widger Tolstoy Busch
Darwin Thoreau Scott
Potter Freud Zola Twain Plato
Lawrence
Kant Jowett Stevenson Dickens
Andersen Burton Hesse Harte
London Descartes Cervantes
Poe Aristotle Wells Voltaire
Hale James Hastings Cooke
Bunner Shakespeare
Richter Chambers Irving
Chekhov da Shaw
Doré Swift Dante Wodehouse Benedict Alcott
Pushkin
Newton

tredition®

tredition was established in 2006 by Sandra Latusseck and Soenke Schulz. Based in Hamburg, Germany, tredition offers publishing solutions to authors and publishing houses, combined with worldwide distribution of printed and digital book content. tredition is uniquely positioned to enable authors and publishing houses to create books on their own terms and without conventional manufacturing risks.

For more information please visit: www.tredition.com

TREDITION CLASSICS

This book is part of the TREDITION CLASSICS series. The creators of this series are united by passion for literature and driven by the intention of making all public domain books available in printed format again - worldwide. Most TREDITION CLASSICS titles have been out of print and off the bookstore shelves for decades. At tredition we believe that a great book never goes out of style and that its value is eternal. Several mostly non-profit literature projects provide content to tredition. To support their good work, tredition donates a portion of the proceeds from each sold copy. As a reader of a TREDITION CLASSICS book, you support our mission to save many of the amazing works of world literature from oblivion. See all available books at www.tredition.com.

Project Gutenberg

The content for this book has been graciously provided by Project Gutenberg. Project Gutenberg is a non-profit organization founded by Michael Hart in 1971 at the University of Illinois. The mission of Project Gutenberg is simple: To encourage the creation and distribution of eBooks. Project Gutenberg is the first and largest collection of public domain eBooks.

Elegies and Other Small Poems

Matilda Betham

Imprint

This book is part of TREDITION CLASSICS

Author: Matilda Betham
Cover design: Buchgut, Berlin – Germany

Publisher: tredition GmbH, Hamburg - Germany
ISBN: 978-3-8424-4476-8

www.tredition.com
www.tredition.de

The intention of the TREDITION CLASSICS series is to make world literature in the public domain available in printed format. Literary enthusiasts and organizations, such as Project Gutenberg, worldwide have scanned and digitally edited the original texts. tredition has subsequently formatted and redesigned the content into a modern reading layout. Therefore, we cannot guarantee the exact reproduction of the original format of a particular historic edition. Please also note that no modifications have been made to the spelling, therefore it may differ from the orthography used today.

ELEGIES AND OTHER SMALL POEMS

BY MATILDA BETHAM.

To the Hon. LADY JERNINGHAM.

Madam,

The many endearing instances of regard I have experienced since I had the honor of being known to your Ladyship, while they impress my mind with gratitude, flatter my hopes with a favourable reception of the following miscellanies, which, under your patronage, I venture to submit to the public.

Considered as the first essays of an early period of life, and as the exercises of leisure, my wishes suggest, that they may not, perhaps, be found wholly unworthy of attention; but whatever be their fate with others, I shall feel myself much gratified, if, in your Ladyship's judgment, they may be allowed some merit.

Though there cannot be a greater pleasure than dwelling on the excellencies of a distinguished and amiable character, I know not that it would be permitted me to indulge my present inclination with enumerating those virtues and endowments which confessedly distinguish your Ladyship, but my wishes I may offer, and that you may long, very long, continue to bless your family, to adorn your rank, and console the unhappy, is the sincere prayer of

Your Ladyship's most obliged humble servant, MATILDA BETHAM.

Stonham, Nov. 20, 1797.

TO THE READER.

If, in the following pages, there may be found any unacknowledged imitations, I hope I shall not be censured as an intentional plagiarist; for it has been my wish, however I may be esteemed presumptuous, not to be unjust; and I sometimes fear lest an imperfect recollection of another's idea should have appeared to me as a dawning thought of my own. Wherever I could recollect a similar passage, although unnoticed at the time I wrote, it has been either altered or acknowledged.

I commit these trifles to the press with the anxiety necessarily resulting from a desire that they may not be deemed altogether worthless. Though the natural partiality of the writer may be somewhat strengthened by the commendations of friends and parents, I am well aware that no apology can give currency to imperfection.

I have not vainly attempted to ascend to the steeps of Parnassus. If, wandering at its foot, I have mistaken perishable shrubs for never-dying flowers, the errors of a youthful mind, first viewing the fascinating regions of fancy, will not be rigidly condemned; for wherever there is true taste, there will be genuine candour.

To – – WITH ARTHUR and ALBINA.

1794.

Ah! if your eye should e'er these lines survey,
Dismiss from thence its penetrating ray:
Let Criticism then her distance keep,
And dreaded Justice then be lull'd to sleep;
For, let whatever sentence be their due,
I feel I cannot censure bear from you.

A British Maid awaits the arrival of her lover from the battle, on a hill, where, at its commencement, she had retired to make vows to heaven for his success. – Evening.

ARTHUR and ALBINA.

Ah me! the yellow western sky turns pale,
And leaves the cheerless sons of earth to mourn;
And yet I hear net in the silent vale,
A sound to tell me Arthur does return.

Ah, haste ye hours! quick plume the loit'ring wing!
Bring back my hero, crown'd with glorious spoils!
Let bards on lofty harps his triumphs sing,
And loud applause repay successful toils!

Reward the flame, ye great celestial pow'rs,
The noble flame that in his bosom glows!
Inspire him, Druids, from your holy bow'rs,
With strength to conquer iron-breasted foes!1

With heighten'd vigour brace his nervous arm,
And let his lance with ten-fold fury fly,
Make him terrific by some potent charm,
And add new lightening to his piercing eye!

Then may my lover gain unrivall'd fame,
The Roman banners may less proudly flow,
Then he may humble their detested name,
And their high plumes wave o'er' a British brow!

Then may his chariot,2 wheeling o'er the plain,
Hurl death and desolation all around,
While his intrepid front appals their train,
And make our proud invaders bite the ground!

But yet I hear no lively foot advance;
No sound of triumph greets my list'ning ear!'
And I may carve this eagle-darting lance
For one, whose voice I never more shall hear!

Perhaps my vows have never reach'd the skies,
Nor heav'n, propitious, smil'd upon my pray'r;
And ah! to morrow's crimson dawn may rise
To plunge me in the horrors of despair!

Yet well he knows the dreadful spear to wield—
Alas! their fearful limbs are fenc'd with care:
And, what can valour, when th'extended shield3
May leave, so oft, his gen'rous bosom bare?

Say, reverend Druids, can you bless in vain?
Can you in vain extend your spotless hands?
Will not heav'n listen when its priests complain,
And save its altars from unhallow'd bands?

Oh yes! I'll fear no more! The sacred groves,4
That rear their untouch'd branches to the skies;

Beneath whose shade its chosen servant roves,
Hidden from weak, unconsecrated eyes:

Beneath whose shade the choral bards rehearse,
Piercing, with uprais'd eyes, each mist that shrouds,
And, listening, catch the heav'n-dictated verse,
By airs etherial wailed from the clouds:

It ne'er can be—but hark! I hear the sound
Of some one's step; yet not the youth I love;
He would have flown, and scarcely touch'd the ground,
Not ling'ring thus, with weary caution, move.

The heavy wanderer approaches nigh,
But the drear darkness skreens him from my views
Ah, gracious heav'n! it was my Arthur's sigh,
Which the unwilling breeze so faintly blew.

Oh speak! inform me what I have to fear!
Speak, and relieve my doubting, trembling heart!
To thy Albina, with a tongue sincere,
A portion of thy wretchedness impart!"

"Sweet maid," replied the wounded, dying youth,
In accents mournful, tremulous and slow,
"Yes, I will ever answer thee with truth,
While yet the feeble tide of life shall flow.

We made the haughty Roman chiefs retire,
The tow'ring, sacrilegious eagle[5] flew;
Our bosoms swell'd with more than mortal fire,
When from the field indignant they withdrew.

But ill bespeaks my faint and languid tongue,
The glowing beauties of that joyful sight;
Ill can my breast, with keenest torture wrung,
Dwell on the charming terrors of the fight.

To others then I leave the envied strain,
Which shall for ages rend the British air;
Nor will thy partial ear expect, in vain,
To find the humble name of Arthur there.

I go, while now the victory is warm,
The just reward of valour to obtain;
Soon I return, clad in a nobler form,[6]
Again to triumph, and again be slain.

Ah! then, my dear Albina, cease to grieve,
Nor at thy lover's glorious fate repine;
For, though my present favour'd form I leave,
This constant heart shall still be only thine.

Alas! e'en now I feel the icy hand

Of hasty death, press down my swelling heart;
E'en now I hear a sweet aerial band,
Summon thy faithful Arthur to depart.

Let not thy tears an absent lover mourn,
Remember that he bravely, nobly died;
Remember that he quickly will return,
And claim again his lov'd, his destin'd bride."

As thus the warrior's fainting spirits fled,
And parting life streamed forth at every vein,
His quivering lip, in whispers, softly said,
"Remember, Arthur dies to live again!"

"Oh stay, dear youth!" the hapless maiden cries,
My best-lov'd Arthur, but one moment stay!
And close not yet those all-enlivening eyes,
So lately lighted at the torch of day.

Ah! yet once more, that look of tender love,
Of fond regret, my Arthur, let me view!
Let one more effort thy affection, prove,
And bid me once, once more, a long adieu.

Now, ere the moon withdraws her feeble light,
Ope yet again on me thy fading eye!
He hears not! memory has ta'en her flight,

And vanish'd with that last convulsive sigh.

Why did I variegated wreaths prepare,
To pay the conqueror every honor due?
Or, why, with fillets, bind my flowing hair,
And tinge my arms of the bright azure hue?7

Oh! must this constant bosom beat no more?
This skilful hand no more direct the spear?
Must lost Albina still her fate deplore,
And ever drop the unavailing tear?

Must I no more that lovely face review,
Expressing each emotion of the mind?
No more repeat a sweetly sad adieu?
No more gay chaplets on his forehead bind?

His forehead, high and fair, with martial grace,
And bold, free curls of glossy chesnut crown'd;
The full, dark eye-brow which adorn'd his face,
O'erwhelming foes with terror as he frown'd.

His voice, though strong, harmoniously clear,
No more shall fill Albina with delight;
No more shall sooth her still-attentive ear,
And make her fancy every sorrow light.

Farewell to love, to happiness, and joy!
Yet will I cull the summer's choicest bloom;
Funereal chaplets shall my time employ,
And wither daily on my Arthur's tomb."

As thus she mourn'd, with bitterest woe opprest,
A ray of light illumin'd all the grove,
And a consoling voice the fair addrest,
In the soft accents of parental love.

Though still she clasp'd her hero's valued corse,
She slowly rais'd her languid, streaming eyes,
And own'd astonishment's resistless force,
Viewing the stranger with a wild surprize.

The form was clad in robes of purest white,
That swept with solemn dignity the ground;
Contrasting with the blackest gloom of night,
Which reign'd in awful majesty around.

The silver beard did reverence demand,8
And told her that a holy bard was there,
Whose shrivell'd fingers grasp'd a flaming brand,
Which threw a lustre on the waving hair.

His eye possess'd the brilliant fire of youth,
United with the wisdom of the sage;

And speaking, with the simple voice of truth,
He blended the solemnity of age.

"Arise! thou loveliest of misfortune's train,
And cease these weak, desponding tears to shed;
The soft effusions of thy grief restrain,
Which serve but to disturb the peaceful dead.

The youth you mourn, far from these scenes of woe,
To worlds of never-ending joy is flown;
Where his blest bosom with delight shall glow,
And his fair temples wear a princely crown.

Ah then, presumptuous! question not the skies,
Nor more with vain laments his loss deplore;
Attend to this, and cease your fruitless sighs,
You soon shall meet where you can part no more."9

Awe-struck, his sacred wisdom she confest,
Which pour'd sweet consolation on her mind;
She cross'd her blood-stain'd hands upon her breast,
And bow'd her humble, grateful head, resign'd.

AUGUST 27, 1794.

1: Alluding to the armour of the Romani.

2: The Britons fought in low chariots, which they could leave and re-ascend at pleasure.

3: The shield being their only armour, when held out to protect a wounded or dying friend, left them defenceless.

4: The groves were consecrated to the celebration of religious mysteries.

5: The Roman standard.

6: The Druids are said to have preached the doctrine of transmigration, in order to inspire their warriors with the greater contempt of death.

7: The practice of staining themselves with blue was common among the Britons.

8: The people, excepting the priests, shaved off all the hair from their faces, but what grew on the upper lip.

9: This equivocal manner of speech may be supposed natural enough in one of this order of priests, who, it is said, held a more refined idea of a future state than they preached to the people.

Alas! no more that joyous morn appears
That led the tranquil hours of spotless fame;
For I have steep'd a father's couch in tears,

SHENSTONE.

THE FRATERNAL DUEL.

'Oh! hide me from the sun! I loath the sight!
I cannot bear his bright, obtrusive ray:
Nought is so dreadful to my gloom as light!
Nothing so dismal as the blaze of day!

No more may I its sparkling glories view!
No more its piercing lustre meet my eye!
On night's black wings my only comfort flew;
At breath of morn I sicken and I die.

Where can I fly? In what sequester'd clime
Does darkness ever hold her ebon reign?
Where woeful dirges measure out the time,
And endless echoes breathe the sullen strain.

Where dreary mountains rear their low'ring heads,
To pierce the heavy and umbrageous clouds;
And where the cavern dewy moisture sheds,
And night's thick veil the guilty mourner shrouds.

There, lost in horrors, I might vent my sighs;
To open misery myself resign;
Might snatch each torturing vision ere it flies,
And feast on prospects desolate as mine.

Oh! let me thither quickly take my flight,

And chuse a favourite and a final seat,
In scenes which would each gentler mind affright,
But for my guilt affords a fit retreat.

There, where no ray, no gleam of light could come,
There, and there only, could I find relief;
There might I ruminate on Edward's doom,
And lose myself in luxury of grief.

And, as it is, though joys around me shine,
Though pleasure here erects her dazzling brow,
Wrapt in despondence, will I droop and pine,
And tears of anguish shall for ever flow.

Oh Edward! could'st thou see this alter'd frame,
Which youthful graces lately did adorn!
Could'st thou behold, and think me still the same,
Thy once gay friend, thus hapless and forlorn?

The cheek, so late by ruddy health embrown'd,
Now pale and faded with incessant tears;
The eye, which once elate, disdain'd the ground,
Now sunk and languid in its orb appears.

Oh! never, never will I cease to grieve!
And sure repentance pardon may obtain!
Can woe unfeign'd incite heav'n to relieve

A wretch opprest with agonizing pain?

Ah no! my hands are stain'd with brother's blood!
A father's curses load my sinking head!
I wish to die, but dare not pass the flood,
For there, as well as here, my hopes are fled.

Sleep, which was meant to chase away the thought,
To lull the sound of dissonant despair,
Appears to me with added terrors fraught,
And my torn heart can find no refuge there.

If, for a moment, I its fetters wear,
And its soft pressure these pale eyes controul,
I injur'd Emma's just reproaches hear,
Or Edward's form appals my shrinking soul.

When in those transitory sleeps I lie,
I oft his beauteous, bleeding form review;
A mild, benignant lustre lights his eye,
As come to bid a friend a last adieu.

I start, I shudder at his tuneful voice,
When it, in soothing whispers, meets my ear;
That sound, which oft has made my heart rejoice,
I now all-trembling and affrighted hear.

Was it thy fault, dear, much-lamented youth
If lovely Emma did thy suit prefer?
She saw thee form'd of tenderness and truth,
And kings might glory to be lov'd by her.

Thy native sweetness won her artless heart;
And well our different characters she knew;
Whilst thy mild looks did happiness impart,
She saw the murderer in each glance I threw.

Yet for this, meanly, did I thee upbraid,
And basely urg'd an elder brother's right;
Then, calling impious passion to my aid,
Forc'd thee, unwilling, to the fatal fight.

Oh! ne'er shall I forget the dreadful hour,
I sheath'd my weapon in thy noble breast;
Thy dying hand clasp'd mine, with feeble pow'r,
And to thy mangled bosom fondly prest.

Whilst o'er thee, I, in speechless anguish hung,
Thou saw'st the wild distraction of my eye;
And, though the chills of death restrain'd thy tongue
Thy bosom heav'd a sympathetic sigh.

With cruel tenderness my friends contriv'd,
To bear me from the drear, polluted shore;

Of every joy, of peace itself depriv'd,
Which this despairing breast shall know no more.

Since this what frenzy has inspir'd my mind!
My tortur'd mem'ry cannot it retrace;
No relique now of former days I find,
But horrors, which e'en madness can't efface.

My dearest brother, and my tenderest friend,
O come, and save me from this dark abyss!
Draw hence the darts which my rack'd bosom rend!
And bear me with you to the realms of bliss!

Ah! whence that pang which smote my shuddering heart?
Where now, for refuge, can lost Anselm fly?
'Tis Death! I know him by his crimson dart!
And, am I fit? Oh heav'ns! I cannot die!

My spirit is not form'd for rapid flight;
It cannot cut the vast expanse of air,
No, never can it reach the realms of light,
For sin, a weight immoveable, lies there!'

Thus wretched Anselm rav'd: unhappy youth!
Though passion hurried thee so far astray,
Thy infant soul ador'd the God of Truth,
And virtue usher'd in thy vernal day.

Oh! had he learn'd his passions to restrain,
And let cool reason in his breast preside,
His op'ning wisdom had not bloom'd in vain,
Nor had he, ere the prime of manhood, died.

Yet, if remorse could expiate his guilt,
If the worst sufferings could the crime erase,
If tears could wash away the blood he spilt,
Then Anselm's penitence obtain'd him grace.

AUGUST 20, 1794.

IN A

LETTER to A.R.C.

ON HER WISHING TO BE CALLED ANNA.

Forgive me, if I wound your ear,
By calling of you Nancy,
Which is the name of my sweet friend,
The other's but her fancy.

Ah, dearest girl! how could your mind
The strange distinction frame?
The whimsical, unjust caprice,
Which robs you of your name.

Nancy agrees with what we see,
A being wild and airy;
Gay as a nymph of Flora's train,
Fantastic as a fairy.

But *Anna's* of a different kind,
A melancholy maid;
Boasting a sentimental soul,
In solemn pomp array'd.

Oh ne'er will I forsake the sound,
So artless and so free!
Be what you will with all mankind.
But *Nancy* still with me.

THE LONELY WALK,

To W.S.B.

When the grey evening spreads a calm around,
Tell me, has thy bewilder'd fancy sought,
Retir'd in some sequestered spot of ground,
Rest, from the labour of eternal thought?

When, wrapt in self, the soul enjoys repose,
The wearied brain resigns its fervent heat,
In dream-like musing every care we lose,
And wind our way with slowly-moving feet.

Oft, to indulge the thought-exploded sig,
When, slowly wandering at the close of day,
Light emanations from th'abstracted eye,

With transient beauty in the sun-beams play,

Thy sister seeks the solitary shade.
Her mind inhaling the aerial gloom,
Sees, not-observing, the fair landscape fade,
And sullen mist usurping day-light's room.

Not her's the feelings which regret inspires,
When sorrows keen have made the spirits low;
Adversity has damp'd the youthful fires,
And all the tears that fall are tears of woe.

Ah no! possessing every social bliss,
I cannot, will not at my fate repine;
Or ask for happiness excelling this,
When such a world of treasures now are mine!

And, when the melancholy grove I seek,
Scarce can my palpitating heart controul,
While silent tears are trembling on my cheek,
The flood of pleasure swelling in my soul.

But soon my too-elated thoughts are calm,
The tumults of the mental chaos cease;
A soft oblivion the rais'd senses charm,
And lull to a reflecting, soothing peace.

Hail, sweet enhancements of the languid mind!
Whose calm reposes restless worldlings scorn;
But from whose aid recruited strength we find,
And waken, lively as the bird of morn.

And thou, lov'd boy, in whose congenial breast,
I doubt not but those sentiments reside;
For we, our thoughts, our actions have confest,
As much in hearts as persons are allied;

Hail thou, my brother! may thy steps be led
By heav'nly wisdom through this world of care,
And gain the realms for which our Saviour, bled!
Nor pain, nor lassitude await us there.

OCTOBER 13, 1794.

The first Percy, who came over with William the Conqueror, married a Saxon lady, called Emma de Port, said to have been the daughter of the last Saxon Earl of Northumberland, whose possessions had been given to him (Lord William de Percy) for his services.

I have taken the liberty of supposing this lady to have had a brother.

THE OUTLAW.

Before the fair Aurora spread
Her azure mantle o'er the skies,
While sleep its pleasing influence shed,
On grateful mortals weary eyes,

Emerg'd from a surrounding wood,
On a bleak mountain's sullen brow,
A solitary outlaw stood,
And view'd, through mist, the world below.

With deep regret his bosom fraught,
His arms were wreath'd in sorrow's knot[10];
Nor seem'd he yet, by patience taught,
To bear submissively his lot.

Hidden was each enlivening grace;
Deprest by his untimely doom;
A hectic flush o'erspread his face,
Instead of nature's florid bloom.

Untutor'd in the school of grief,
His pining spirit spoke in sighs;
Though almost hopeless of relief,
He look'd around with eager eyes;

And fondly bent an anxious ear,
To the slow murmuring of the breeze,
Essaying oft, in vain, to hear
A friendly step beneath the trees.

"Delusive wish!" at last he cried,
"Why wilt thou fill my aching breast?
And thus my miseries deride,
By telling how I might be blest.

"No kind consolers hither bend,
By sympathy to ease my care;
Here comes no ever-faithful friend,
Who yet might shield me from despair.

"The abbey's well-known tow'r I seek,
It fades from my impassion'd eye;
The fancied outlines softly break,
And melt into the distant sky.

"No pitying object now remains,
That I may know those scenes are near,
Where generous love and friendship reigns,
And Alwin's name may claim a tear.

"And you, my lov'd paternal groves,

Where I no more must shew my head;
In your fair walks a stranger roves,
And treacherous Normans daily tread!

"E'en now their presence may prophane
The halls where Herbert did reside!
E'en now may joy and gladness reign,
And Adelaide be Percy's bride.

"Yet no! her soul, the seat of truth,
Would ne'er a second love receive!
The sacred vows of artless youth,
Her Alwin ever shall believe!

"They still shall comfort my sad heart,
And sooth the anguish of my mind;
Shall still a cheering hope impart,
And make me somewhat more resign'd.

"Ah! yet I hear her trembling hand,
Withdraw the bolt to set me free!
Yet hear the hasty, kind command,
My Alwin fly, and live for me!

"No other can obtain my love!
I would for thee the world resign!
Then let thy prompt obedience prove

That thou art truly, wholly mine."

"And ever to her promise true,
No pleasure shall her soul elate,
For, yet her constant thoughts pursue
A wretched Outlaw's hapless fate!

"In vain proud Ranulph[11] shall upbraid,
My Adelaide is still the same!
And, for thy sake, dear, lovely maid,
I will not curse the Norman name!

"Not, though my father's large domains,
Are plunder'd by the murderous bands;
And my Northumbria's fertile plains,
Lie wasted by their cruel hands;

"Though, as a son, I mourn the fate
Of those, to whom my life I owe;
And hate the hearts that thus create
The dimness of severest woe;

"Though I behold no friendly steel,
To give my Emma vengeance, drawn;
And though a brother's pangs I feel,
To know her destitute, forlorn;

"Though, banish'd from the sight of day,
In dreary solitude I pine;
And, forc'd to feel a tyrant's sway,
Each dear paternal right resign;

"Yet will I seal my lips; nor dare
To extricate my haughty foes:
The hateful, guilty root I spare,
Which can produce so fair a rose.

"But thou, my heart, wilt thou be calm?
Oh! tell me, can reflection cease;
And this fond bosom, now so warm,
Be ever tranquilliz'd to peace!

"Ah, no! a father's scornful eye
Is ever present to my view;
And tells me, Herbert dar'd to die,
Though Normans could his son subdue.

"Each feeble plea his soul disdains,
They cannot for the fault atone;
Though, when I left Northumbria's plains,
I had not fifteen summers known.

"And hear me, Herbert, when I swear
It was not fear that urg'd my flight;

A worthless life was not my care,
I thought but of a parent's right.

"Then pardon that my youth comply'd,
To ease a mother's anxious fears
That, when I rather would have died,
I yielded to a sister's tears.

"Alas! a peasant's humble shed,
Soon saw our sainted parents' death,
Who, while our hearts in anguish bled,
With pious hopes resign'd her breath.

"When mists foretel the ev'ning near,
And clouds of chilling dew arise,
We sought the grave of her so dear,
And offer'd there our tears and sighs.

"'Till mild reflection lent her aid,
And bade our filial sorrows cease;
The fever of our souls allay'd,
We sunk into a mournful peace.

"My pensive bosom strove to keep
A dying mother's last request;
I let the thoughts of vengeance sleep,
And studied to make Emma blest.

"No longer shunning of the dawn,
Or seeking the sequester'd shade,
I call'd my sister to the lawn,
And trod with her the flow'ry glade.

"Submitting to our wayward fate,
I talk'd not of the treasures flown;
But still seem'd easy and sedate,
While pressing verdure not my own.

"Then all I wish'd, and all I fear'd,
Was by fraternal love inspir'd;
And one, by every tie endear'd,
The only friend my soul desir'd.

"Yet soon that pleasing calmness fled,
A Norman beauty won my heart,
Imperious love my footsteps led,
And bade all secrecy depart.

"I own'd the splendour of my race,
Altho' a peasant's form I bore;
I fancied silence was disgrace,
And hid my sentiments no more.

"Her father's tongue my fate decreed,

And doom'd great Herbert's son to shame;
For, tho' by love from prison freed,
I bear an outlaw's hateful name.

"My sister no fond friend can shield,
No relative allay her grief;
For tyranny all hearts hath steel'd,
And nought can give her soul relief.

"With ev'ry quality to charm,
A guardian will not heaven allow,
To screen thy artless youth from harm,
And, fair deserted! help thee now!

"No aid, no comfort, can be nigh!
And shall thy brother here remain?
Has he not fortitude to fly,
And burst the heavy, servile chain?

"Why should I linger here alone,
Unseen by every human eye?
To live unfriended and unknown,
And in this dreary desart die.

"For now the sun-beams gild the sky,
And give the misty morning grace,
Far from the light I'm doom'd to fly,

Abandon'd by the human race.

"But no! I'll bear suspense no more!
Too dear a price to purchase breath;
I'll seek the scenes I yet deplore,
And meet a welcome, wish'd-for, death."

Tortur'd to frenzy, Alwin flew,
And as he left his sad retreat,
He, turning, look'd a last adieu,
And shook the dew-drops from his feet.

His hurried steps nor press'd the ground,
Nor pointed out the path he came;
And, though so long the way he found,
Despair buoy'd up his fainting frame.

The sun shot forth a feeble ray,
But hid his glorious orb from sight,
And the pale evening's modest grey,
Had soften'd the too-glaring light,

When Alwin reach'd the humble cot,
That once he did with Emma share,
And, weeping, hail'd the well-known spot,
In vain, for Emma was not there.

Repuls'd, he turn'd his languid eye,
Where Ranulph's lofty turrets rose;
And, heaving disappointment's sigh,
He sought the mansion of his foes.

His faltering step, when there he came,
A proud, disdainful air possest;
Memory recall'd his former shame,
And indignation fill'd his breast.

He enter'd, in his wild attire,
With hasty pace and haggard brow,
Scorn fill'd his azure eye with fire,
And gave his cheeks a deeper glow.

A graceful knight who met his view,
Sat pleading by a lady's side;
And Alwin's jealous bosom knew
Lord Percy, and his fated bride.

Mistaken youth! thy eyes have seen,
The persons pictur'd in thy mind;
But who is that, with pensive mien,
And forehead on her hand reclin'd?

O'er whom Lord Ranulph fondly bends,
With sorrow seated on his brow;

While the regretting tear descends
O'er his pale cheek, in silent woe.

"Ah! is it thus?" sad Alwin said,
The fancied bride the accents knew,
Lord Percy rais'd his drooping head,
And lovely Emma met his view.

Then rapture and surprize prevail'd,
Each bosom felt confus'd delight;
While his return the mourner hail'd,
And thus his sorrows did requite.

"O, dearest Alwin, now no more
My father disapproves our flame;
No longer we thy loss deplore,
Or tremble to pronounce thy name.

"A noble friend has gain'd our cause,
And vanquish'd all his former hate;
Who, ere he own'd a lover's laws,
With generous tears had wept thy fate."

"Yes, injur'd youth," Lord Ranulph cried,
"Thou art this day my chosen heir;
In Adelaide behold thy bride,
Thy sister's future husband, there.

"Lord Percy, to a candid mind,
Unites a fervour like thy own;
And Emma, not to merit blind,
Refers his cause to thee alone.

"If thou wilt grant his fond desire,
'Twill gain a brave, a noble friend;
And the possessions of thy sire,
To his posterity descend."

"And did my Emma stay to hear,
Her brother sanctify her choice?
Ah Percy! now you need not fear
From Alwin, a dissenting voice.

"Blest in my love, in Emma blest,
My heart each cherish'd wish obtains;
Northumbrians, now no more opprest,
Shall own a son of Herbert reigns.

"May ye rebuild the peasant's cot,
Exalt the woe-depressed head,
And o'er each desolated spot,
The fostering calm of quiet spread!

"May sterne reserve and caution cease!

With lenient hand dispense your sway;
Give them the healing balm of peace,
Their wounded spirits will obey.

"Ah! cheer their gloom! dispel their care!
The smile will soon replace the tear;
And, wedded to a Saxon fair,
The foreign lord no more appear."

1794.

10: "Wreathing his arms in this sad knot."—SHAKESPERE'S TEMPEST.

11: Lord of Cumberland.

INVITATION,

To J.B.C.

Now spring appears, with beauty crown'd,
And all is light and life around,
Why comes not Jane? When friendship calls,
Why leaves she not Augusta's walls?
Where cooling zephyrs faintly blow,
Nor spread the cheering, healthful glow.
That glides through each awaken'd vein,
As skimming o'er the spacious plain,

We look around with joyous eye,
And view no boundaries but the sky.

Already April's reign is o'er,
Her evening tints delight no more;
No more the violet scents the gale,
No more the mist o'erspreads the vale;
The lovely queen of smiles and tears,
Who gave thee birth, no more appears;
But blushing May, with brow serene,
And vestments of a livelier green,
Commands the winged choir to sing,
And with wild notes the meadows ring.

O come! ere all the train is gone,
No more to hail thy twenty-one;
That age which higher honor shares,
And well becomes the wreath it wears.
From lassitude and cities flee,
And breathe the air of heav'n, with me.

MAY 5, 1795.

WRITTEN ON

WHITSUN-MONDAY,

1795.

At an open window sitting,
On this day of mirth and glee,
'Cross a flow'ry vista flitting,
Many passing forms I see.
Ah! lovely prospect, stay awhile!
And longer glad my doating eye,
With poverty's delighted smile,
And lighten'd step, as passing by;

With labour's spruce and ruddy train,
Deck'd out in all their best array,
Who, months of toil and care disdain,
Paid by the pleasures of a day.
The village girl still let me view,
Hast'ning to the neighb'ring fair;
Her cap adorn'd with pink or blue,
And nicely smooth her glossy hair.

With sparkling eye and smiling face,
Ting'd o'er with beauty's warmest glow;
With timid air, and Rumble grace,
With clear and undepressed brow.
Go! lovely girl, and share the day,

To thy industrious merit due;
There join the dance, or choral lay;
Thou blooming, village rose, adieu!

And thou, O youth, so blythe and free,
Bounding swiftly o'er the plain,
Go, taste the joys of liberty,
And cheer thy spirit, happy swain!
How different to the lonely hour,
When slowly following the plough,
Self-buoyant joy forgets the pow'r,
Which warms thy gladden'd bosom now.

If some rural prize desiring,
Or ambitious of applause,
Loud huzzas thy wishes firing,
Thy steady hand the furrow draws;
Ne'er a victor fam'd in story,
Greater praise and reverence drew,
Than thou, attir'd in humble glory,
So, guiltless conqueror, adieu!

Oh, here a charming group appears!
A cottage family, so gay,
Whose youthful hopes, uncheck'd by fears,
In smiles of thoughtless rapture play.
Here, borne in fond, parental arms,

The infant's roving eye we view;
Boasting a thousand, thousand charms,
Endearing innocents, adieu!

They go! no more with beating heart,
And lively, dancing step to tread;
Unwillingly will they depart,
To seek again their homely shed.
Ah! Eve, I love thy veil of grey,
Which will conceal them from my view,
For, bending home their weary way,
How sad would be our last adieu!

The following was suggested by reading a whimsical description, given by Scarron, of the deformity of his person, contrasted with its former elegance, in the Curiosities of Literature, vol. 2, page 247.

PHILEMON.

Ye blooming youth, possest of every grace,

Which can delight the eye, or please the ear,
Who boast a polish'd mind and faultless face,
Awhile the councils of Philemon hear!

Let not pride lift the thoughtless head too high,
Temerity arch o'er the scornful brow,
Contemptuous glances arm the sparkling eye,
Or the high heart with self-complacence glow!

Alas! full soon the eve of life arrives,
Though pale Disease's train approach not nigh;
Short is the summer of the happiest lives,
If no rude storm disturbs the smiling sky.

This wretched body, bending to the earth,
Once, on the wings of health, alert and gay,
Shone forth the foremost in the train of mirth,
And cloudless skies announc'd a beauteous day.

My parents oft, with fond complacence view'd,
The elegance of my external form;
And thought my mind with excellence endued,
Bright as my genius, as my fancy warm.

There was a time, poor as I now appear,
I admiration met in every look;
And, harsh as now my words may grate your ear,

Each tongue was silent when Philemon spoke.

Once could this voice make every bosom thrill,
As it pour'd forth the light or plaintive lay;
And once these fingers, with superior skill,
Upon the lute could eloquently play.

By partial friendship sooth'd, by flattery fann'd,
I learnt with conscious grace the dance to lead,
To guide the Phaeton with careless hand,
And rule, with flowing rein, the prancing steed.

Sick with the glory of a trifler's fame,
By folly nurtur'd, I was proud and vain;
Till Chastisement in kindest mercy came,
Though then her just decrees I dar'd arraign.

The form that sought so late the public view,
That glow'd with transport, as the world admir'd,
Fill'd with false shame, from every eye withdrew,
And to the shades of solitude retir'd.

Consum'd by fevers, spiritless, forlorn,
Blasted by apoplexy's dreadful rage,
My bleeding heart by keen remembrance torn,
I past my prime in premature old age.

I heard my parent's ill-suppressed sighs,
And wish'd myself upon the peaceful bier;
I saw the anguish of their sleepless eyes,
The smile dissembled, and the secret tear.

Oft, with a kind of gratifying woe,
I recollected every former charm,
And, with the spleen of a malicious foe,
Delighted still to keep my sorrows warm.

"Where is the lustre of the gladsome eye,
The airy smile, the animated mien,
The rounding lip of liveliest crimson dye,
So lately envied, now no longer seen.

"I too have gloried in my waving hair,
No ringlets now remain to raise my pride;
Nor can I now lay the white forehead bare,
And push the too luxuriant locks aside."

Thus, like a child, I sigh'd for pleasures past,
And lost my hours in a delusive dream;
But Reason op'd my blinded eyes at last,
And clear'd each mist by her refulgent beam.

I saw futurity before me spread,
A scourge or sceptre offer'd to my view,

Alarm'd, from Folly's erring mazes fled,
And to my God with humble rev'rence drew.

I bow'd, submissive, at the holy shrine,
His mercy with warm gratitude confest,
Which had reveal'd the spark of life divine,
That slumber'd in my earth-enamoured breast.

Had I, as friendship and self-love desir'd,
Still suck'd delirium at the fane of praise,
I might, my conscience lull'd and passions fir'd,
Have lost my soul in the bewitching blaze.

Dear rising train, let not my words offend!
Nor the pure dictates of my love despise;
To one, late like yourselves, attention lend,
And, taught by his experience, be wise!

Ah! banish from your eye the fiend Disdain;
Let fair simplicity supply its place;
Nor longer let conceit the bosom stain;
The child of weakness, follow'd by disgrace.

Should time from you each glowing beauty wrest,
You will not then those self-reproaches feel,
Which every eye awaken'd in my breast,
And twenty winters scarce suffic'd to heel.

Nor will your friends observe each faded charm,
Since still your countenance its smile retains,
And the same lov'd companion, kind and warm,
With unassuming manners, yet remains.

SEPT. 8, 1795.

ON A FAN.

Now I've painted these flowers, say what can I do,
To render them worthy acceptance from you?
I know of no sybil, whose wonderful art
Could to them superior virtues impart,
Who, of magical influence wonders could tell,
And, who over each blossom could mutter a spell.

You only the humbler enchantments can prove,
That arise from esteem, from respect, and from love;
With such I assail you, and pow'rful the charm,
When applied to a heart sympathetic and warm;
To a heart such as that, which, if right I divine,
O C—ll—n—n! dwells in that bosom of thine.

NOV. 10, 1795.

TO SIMPLICITY.

Fair village nymph, ah! may I meet
Thy pleasing form where'er I stray!
With open air and converse sweet,
Still cheer my undiscover'd way!

With eyes, that shew the placid mind,
And with no feign'd emotions roll;
With mien, that sprightly or resign'd,
Bespeaks the temper of the soul.

With smiles, where not the lips alone
Receive a brighter, vermil hue,
The cheek does warmer roses own,
And the eyes beam, a deeper blue!

Though Fashion's minions scorn thy pow'r,
And slight thee, 'cause in russet drest,
Yet Joy frequents thy peaceful bow'r,
And sorrow flies to thee for rest.

The echoing laugh, the rapturous tear,
The smile of friendship, gay and free,
Delight but when they are sincere,
And given, lovely nymph, by thee.

When my Rosina reads a tale,
Though sweet the tuneful accents flow,
No studied pathos does prevail
To bid the hearer's bosom glow;

Her voice to sympathy resign'd,
Each different feeling can impart.
And, tell me not, we e'er can find
A modulator, like the heart!

And Mary's locks of glossy brown,
That fall in waves, with graceful swell,
In ever-varying ringlets thrown,
The fairest curls of art excel.

Still rob'd in innocence and ease,
Daughter of Truth, shall thou prevail,
When Affectation cannot please,
And all the spells of Fashion fail.

NOV. 17, 1795.

THE TERRORS OF GUILT.

Yon coward, with the streaming hair,
And visage, madden'd to despair,
With step convuls'd, unsettled eye,
And bosom lab'ring with a sigh,
Is *Guilt!*—Behold, he hears the name,
And starts with horror, fear, and shame!

See! slow Suspicion by his side,
With winking, microscopic eye!
And Mystery, his muffled guide,
With fearful speech, and head awry.

See! scowling Malice there attend,
Bold Falsehood, an apparent friend;
Avarice, repining o'er his pelf,
Mean Cunning, lover of himself;
Hatred, the son of conscious Fear,
Impatient Envy, with a fiend-like sneer,
And shades of blasted Hopes, which still are hovering near!

All other woes will find relief,
And time alleviate every grief;
Memory, though slowly, will decay,
And Sorrow's empire pass away.
Awhile Misfortune may controul,
And Fain oppress the virtuous soul,
Yet Innocence can still beguile
The patient sufferer of a smile,
The beams of Hope may still dispense
A grateful feeling to the sense;
Friendship may cast her arms around,
And with fond tears embalm the wound,
Or Piety's soft incense rise,

And waft reflection to the skies;
But those fell pangs which he endures,
Nor Time forgets, nor Kindness cures;
Like Ocean's waves, they still return,
Like Etna's fires, forever burn.

Hound him no genial zephyrs fly,
No fair horizon glads his eye,
No joys to him does Nature yield,
The solemn grove, or laughing field;
Though both with loud rejoicings ring,
No pleasure does the echo bring,
Not bubbling waters as they roll,
Can tranquillize his bursting soul,
For Conscience still, with tingling smart,
Asserts his empire o'er his heart,
And even when his eye-lids close,
With clamourous scream affrights repose.

Oppress'd with light, he seeks to shun
The splendid glories of the sun;
The busy crowds that hover near,
Torment his eye, distract his ear;
He hastens to the secret shades,
Where not a ray the gloom pervades;
Where Contemplation may retreat,
And Silence take his mossy seat;
Yet even there no peace he knows,
His fev'rish blood, no calmer flows;
Some hid assassins 'vengeful knife,
Is rais'd to end his wretched life.
He shudders, starts, and stares around,
With breathless fright, to catch the fancied sound;
Seeks for the dagger in his breast,
And gripes it 'neath his ruffled vest.

Lo! now he plunges in the flood,
To cleanse his garments, stain'd with blood,
His sanguine arm, in terror, laves;
But ah! its hue defies the waves.
Deprest, bewildered, thence he flies,
And, to avoid Detection, tries,
Who, frowning, still before him stands,
The sword of Justice in her hands;
Abhorrent Scorn, unpitying Shame,
And Punishments without a name,
Still on her sounding steps attend,
And every added horror lend.
He turns away, with dread and fear,
But the fell spectres still are near.
Though Falsehood's mazes see him wind!
Yet Infamy is close behind,
Lifting her horn, with horrors fraught,
Whose hideous yell is frenzy to the thought.

Now, maniac-like, he comes again,
And mixes with the jocund train;
But still those eyes that wildly roll,
Bespeak the tempest in his soul.
In yon deep cave he strives to rest,
But Mem'ry harrows up his breast;
He clasps the goblet, foe to Care,
And lo! Distraction hovers there.

Ah, hapless wretch! condemn'd to know,
The sad varieties of woe;
Where'er thy footsteps turn, to meet,
An earthquake yawning at thy feet,
While o'er thy head pale meteors glare,
And boding tempests fill the air,
In throbbing anguish doom'd to roam,
Yet never find a peaceful home.

Haste! to the shrine of Mercy hie,
There lift the penitential eye,
With breaking heart thy sins deplore,
And wound Integrity no more!
Repentance then thy soul shall save,
And snatch thee, ransom'd, from the grave.

JULY 1796.

The death of Selred, last King of the East-Saxons, reduced that part of the Heptarchy to dependance on Mercia. The rest is imaginary.

CEN'LIN, PRINCE OF MERCIA.

When Britain many chiefs obey'd,
And seven Saxon princes sway'd,
The Mercian monarch, fam'd afar,
In peace respected, fear'd in war,
Favour'd by heav'n above the rest,
In his brave son was fully blest;
For none like Cen'lin did arise,
So virtuous, elegant, and wise.

Of partial Mercian eyes the joy,
His parents idoliz'd the boy;
Saw with just pride each op'ning grace,
His charms of mind, of form, and face.

And as he oft, with modest air,
His thoughts and feelings did declare,
His father would delighted hear,
Would fondly drop the grateful tear;
And proudly cast his eyes around,
But not an equal could be found.
Warm from each lip applauses broke,
And every tongue his praises spoke;
The list'ning courtiers spread his fame,
And blessings follow'd Cen'lins name.

Now twenty summer's suns had flown,
And Mercia's hopes were fully blown;
When ah! conceal'd in coarse disguise,
To Selred's12 court their darling flies.
Selred, his father's scorn and hate,
Became the ruler of his fate.
There flatter'd, lov'd, the youth remain'd,
Till Cenulph's threats his heir regain'd.
But ah! no more the son of mirth,
His pensive eye now sought the earth;
No more within the dance to move,
Or list to sages, did he love;
But from surrounding friends would fly,
To pour in solitude the sigh.
And soon again the youth withdrew,
Again to th' Eastern-Saxons flew.
His father heard, opprest with woe,
His aged heart forgot to glow;
He learnt his foes an army led,
With youthful Cen'lin at their head,
He call'd his warriors forth to meet,
And stretch the rebel at hit feet:
Tears from his eyes in anguish broke,
As thus the aged monarch spoke:

"Ye Mercians, let your banners fly!
The graceless youth this day shall die!
For, since he dares an army bring
Against his father and his king,
Though dear as life, I will not spare,
Nor listen to affection's pray'r!
If all my people should implore,
I'll pardon the rash boy no more!
His harden'd heart, to duty blind,
No ties of gratitude can bind;
This hoary head would else have rest,
And pleasure warm this aching breast.
Ah, cruel youth! thy wrongs I feel,
More deep than wounds of pointed steel.
For, if forlorn the parent's doom,
Who bears his offspring to the tomb,
Some comfort still his breast may know,
Some soothing thought may calm his woe,
And when he gives a loose to pain,
He feels not that he mourns in vain,
But fancies still his darling nigh,
And grateful for each bursting sigh,
Still bending o'er, with list'ning ear,
Each weeping, fond complaint to hear,
The dear-lov'd phantom hovers round,
And pours a balm in every wound.

"How doubly poignant is my smart,
Bereaved of my Cen'lin's heart!
Exil'd from that deluded breast,
Where I had fondly hop'd to rest,
With faith undoubting, sweet repose,
Till Death should bid my eye-lids close.
And sometimes yet will hope arise;
Till now he ever scorn'd disguise;
Some cursed fiend might taint his youth,
And warp a temper form'd for truth.

When late he humbly knelt for grace,
And clasp'd my knees in close embrace,
Upon his lips a secret hung,
But something seem'd to stay his tongue;
I prest not, for my anger slept,
And fondness only saw he wept;
Ah! fatal haste! then had I known
The serpent, I had sav'd my son!
Yet surely pardon frank as mine,
A noble heart would more confine!
When leaguing with my bitter foe,
To strike some grand, decisive blow;
Perhaps to rob me of my throne,
And make it, ere the time, his own;
Or, should wan guilt a danger dread,
To humble this devoted head,
Each throbbing pang of conscience drown,
And seize, with bloody hands, the crown.
O'er this offence I cast a veil,
And fondly hush'd the whisper'd tale.
Ah fool! deluded by the grace,
Of that fine form, and perfect face;
I thought his bosom free from sin,
Nor dreamt a demon lurk'd within.
His voice, which ever could controul,
Each passion of the hearer's soul,
With ease my partial heart beguil'd,
Who knew no sorrows when he smil'd.
And ah! my friends, your downcast eyes,
Your pensive air, and smother'd sighs,
All tell me you lament the fate,
Of him, whom yet you cannot hate.
And shall I bear then to behold,
That form inanimate and cold,
His smiling lips depriv'd of breath,
His eyes for ever clos'd in death!
Ah no! my heart with anguish swells,
And every throbbing vein rebels.

Let sorrow weep, or anger thrill,
Yet all the parent triumphs still.

"Oh Father! who in mercy reigns,
If thy all-ruling will ordains,
That my unhappy Cen'lin dies,
Remove the picture from my eyes!
At the same moment set us free,
Both rebel sons, my God, to thee!"
Thus did the king pour forth his pray'r,
With all the wildness of despair;
Then, stilling every rising sigh,
He calm'd the anguish of his eye,
And though within the burthen lay,
He wip'd the falling tears away.

When lo! there comes a youthful train,
Descending swiftly to the plain,
Drest like the fairest sons of day,
In floating robes and colours gay;
No crested helmets there appear,
No glittering shield or pointed spear,
But youths with honey-suckles crown'd,
Or their fair locks with fillets bound,
Whose circling ranks and varied dyes,
Shew'd like the bow, that gilds the skies.
Whilst in the van a pair were seen,
Of peerless charms and graceful mien;
One lovely form the Mercians knew,
And gladden'd at the pleasing view,
Who, with the glow of youthful prime,
Had all the majesty of time.
And beauteous was the fair he led,
As any fabled Grecian maid;
The nymphs who tend Aurora's car,
And usher in the morning star,

Though made inhabitants of air,
Were not more elegant and fair;
Nor Dian's ever-healthful train,
When skimming o'er the spacious plain.
Had not more pure, more lively dyes,
Or brighter lustre in their eyes.

The king, so late by woe deprest,
Felt hope reanimate his breast,
And as his Cen'lin nearer drew,
His waking hopes more vivid grew.
"My friends," he cried, "will you believe,
That open mien can e'er deceive?
That blooming, form can e'er unfold,
A heart ungenerous and cold,
That melting softness of the eye,
Can harbour direst cruelty?
Ah no! a poison's baleful pow'r,
Lurks not beneath so fair a flow'r.
Nor are those youths with amber hair,
Such as fell treason would prepare,
An aged monarch to dethrone,
And hear, unmov'd, a father's groan.
Gay are their looks, no dark disguise,
Dims the mild radiance of their eyes;
No murderous thoughts their souls employ,
But, heralds of transporting joy,
They come to bid suspicion cease,
And sooth my sorrow into peace."
Caution could scarce awhile controul
The strong delights of Cenulph's soul,
When Cen'lin knelt, and by his side
Half-kneeling, bent his lovely bride.
But, when he first essay'd to speak,
A hasty blush pass'd o'er his cheek,
He hung awhile his graceful head,
Till thus, with air confus'd he said:

"I come, by love with honours crown'd,
Yet sorrow casts a shade around,
That when my consort here I bring,
The heiress of a potent king,
The Mercians, clad in armour, come,
To lead their princess to her home.
No joyful hail our nuptial greets,
No proof of love my Ela meets,
But scarlet banners, waving high,
The bridal knot and wreath supply.
Alas! I see mistrust has won
E'en Cenulph's fondness from his son;
Or could my ever-honour'd sire,
A proof of Cen'lin's faith require?
Can force so needful now appear,
To aid a pow'r which I revere?
When eager beauty's form to view,
I first to Selred's court withdrew,
A single wish thy pow'r maintain'd,
A single wish thy son regain'd.
I left the maid whose matchless charms,
Each rooted prejudice disarms,
Who rul'd my heart with sovereign sway,
And taught a Mercian to obey
Laws that East-Saxons can impart,
When wit and beauty string the dart;
Left her when hope my doubts beguil'd,
And on our love her father smil'd.
Oft have I tried to win thine ear,
The fond, romantic tale to hear,
But when I found a lonely hour,
My coward soul has lost the pow'r;
As on my lips the accents hung,
Thy hate to Selred check'd my tongue.
Yet flattering hopes my passion fed,
And from thy court again I fled;
I thought when you my fair beheld,
And knew how greatly she excell'd,

In every charm, each art refin'd,
And virtue of the female mind,
Thy judgment would approve my choice,
And bless it with a cheerful voice.
And ah! though fortune did combine
With love, in making Ela mine,
I cannot from a grief refrain,
Remembering that I gave thee pain.
Yet if thy Cen'lin e'er could please,
If e'er my cares could give thee ease,
Let mild affection now arise,
And beam forgiveness from thine eyes!
No more thy son shall make thee know
A pain, or give thee cause of woe.
No nights the Mercians have to fear,
For all I love is center'd here,"
He spoke, and o'er his father's soul,
A stream of healing comfort stole;
He rose, with slow, majestic grace,
Tears of delight adorn'd his face,
His pious heart with rapture glow'd,
And joy a second youth bestow'd.

"To meet thee thus, my son," he cried,
"This peerless maiden for your bride,
Bids each distressing thought depart,
And joy again possess my heart.
Fair princess, thine the happy fate,
To heal the wounds of mutual hate;
No longer shall this bosom know,
An Eastern-Saxon as my foe;
And she, who bids that passion rest,
Doubt not, shall be supremely blest;
The part is holy and benign,
Befitting such a form as thine.
This day, far dearer than before,
Kind heav'n does twice my son restore,

For by those speaking looks I see,
Another valued child in thee."

As then he raised them to his breast,
Around the joyful Mercians prest,
And made their shouts of triumph rise,
To the fair concave of the skies.

OCTOBER 1795.

12: King of the East-Saxons.

RHAPSODY.

Lo! here a cloud comes sailing, richly clad
In royal purple, which the parting beams
Of bounteous Phoebus edge with tints of gold
And lucid crimson. One might fancy it
A noble bird, that laves its graceful form,
And bathes its rosy bosom in the light.
Look! how it swells and rears its snowy crest
With haughty grandeur; while the blue expanse,
In smiling patience lets the boaster pass,
And swell his train with all the lazy vapours
That hover in the air: an easy prey
To the gigantic phantom, whose curl'd wing,
Sweeps in these worthless triflers of the sky,
And wraps them in his bosom. Go, vain shadow!
Sick with the burthen of thy fancied greatness,
A breath of zephyr wafts thee into nothing,
Scatters thy spreading plumes, uncrowns thy front,
And drives thee downward to thy mother earth,
To mix with vapour and dissolve in dew.

Such are the dreams of hope, which to the eye
Of youthful inexperience, seem to touch
The pure, unclouded sky of certainty.
Buoy'd up by the fond eloquence of thought,
And nurtur'd by the smile of vanity,
Each hour the air-born vision gathers bulk,
And Fancy decks it with a thousand hues,
Varied and wild, till it abounds in charms
Which sink the soul to sadness, when the breath
Of gentle Reason breaks the beauteous bubble,
And leaves us nought but vain regret behind.

FEBRUARY 1, 1797.

HUMAN PLEASURE OR PAIN.

When clouds and rain deform the sky,
And light'nings glare around,
Amidst the dreary, cheerless scene,
Some comfort may be found.

There will, at some far-distant spot,
A streak of light appear,
Or, when the sullen vapours break,
The ether will be clear.

And if the sun illumes the east,

And sheds his gladsome ray,
Some boding mist, or passing cloud
Will threat the rising day.

The heart rejoicing in the view,
And dancing with delight,
Oft feels the touch of palsied fear,
And sinks at thought of night.

So Hope's bright torch more clearly shines,
Amidst surrounding gloom,
And, beldame Fortune vainly throws
Her mantle o'er the tomb.

MARCH 15,1797.

THE COMPLAINT OF FANCY.

To A.R.C.

As, musing, late I sat reclin'd,
And waking dreams absorb'd my mind,
A damsel came, of various dyes,
Like painted Iris from the skies;
A purfled saffron was her vest,

And sweet gum-cistus form'd her crest;
In many a playful ring, her hair
Flew light and flossy in the air;
The mantle, blue and gold, she wore,
A rose of opals held before,
While, graceful in her fairy hand,
Appear'd a crimson-tufted wand,
Whose shade on every object threw
A glowing tint of roseate hue.

"Whence art thou, blooming nymph?" I cried,
And thus a tuneful voice replied:
"Men call me Fancy; at my shrine
Myriads confess my power divine;
There painters bend the willing knee,
And laurell'd poets sue to me:
For mine is every vivid ray,
Which partial Nature gave the day;
And, to the music of my song,
A thousand nameless charms belong.

"The friend of Happiness, I dwell
Belov'd alike in court or cell;
Where Glory lifts her ardent eye,
With hasty, kindred zeal I fly,
In sun-beams place the hero's form,
And bid his arm command the storm;
On swelling clouds an altar raise,
And fan the tow'ring flame of praise.

"Oft, from the lorn enthusiast's lyre,
My fingers strike etherial fire,
And give to sounds of piercing woe,
Extatic rapture's fervent glow.
Oft sooth the maniac's throbbing vein,
And grace her simple, wilder'd strain;

The tribe of Pain in fetters keep,
Lull wounded Memory to sleep,
And, in the mind of gloomy Care,
Bid Thought an angel's semblance wear.

"Dear to each blest aerial pow'r,
E'en Wisdom calls me to her bow'r;
My songs her leisure hours beguile,
And teach her holy lip to smile.
And, when the Muse, with thoughtful care,
Has woven chaplets for her hair,
I let her, with her myrtles, twine,
Full many a fragrant rose of mine.

"Then why, since all the wise and gay,
To me a grateful homage pay,
Since I to all my hand extend,
And, liberal, every heart befriend,
Does Nancy from the croud retire,
And rend my blossoms from her lyre?
Though every string the loss bewail,
And tones of mellow sweetness fail,
Which us'd to charm the pensive ear,
When list'ning Friendship bent to hear.

"Tell her I wish not to intrude
Upon her sacred solitude,
Nor cast my undulating chain,
Around her glowing heart again;
No! every claim I now resign,
Yet let some small regard be mine;
Let one, who nurs'd her infant years,
And wip'd away some bitter tears,
Still animate the scenes around,
And make her tread on fairy ground;
Give playful sweetness to each lay,

And decorate the passing day.

"Tell her, if now she scorns my strain,
She may invoke my name in vain;
In vain my proffered aid implore,
Contemn'd, I hardly pardon more."

She said, and springing from the earth,
Attending found her suitor Mirth,
Who caught her hand, with lively air,
And plac'd her in his silver chair,
Which through the yielding ether flew,
And quickly bore them from my view.

ON THE

EVE OF DEPARTURE

From O— —

Loud beats the rain! The hollow, groan
Of rushing winds I hear,
That with a deep and sullen moan,
Pass slowly by the ear.

Soon will my dying fire refuse
To yield a cheerful ray,
Yet, shivering still I sit and muse
The latest spark away.

Ah, what a night! the chilly air
Bids comfort hence depart,
While sad repining's clammy wings
Cling icy, to my heart.

To-morrow's dawn may fair arise,
And lovely to the view;
The sun with radiance gild the skies,
Yet then—I say adieu!

Oh, stay, dear Night, with cautious care,

And lingering footsteps move,
Though day may be more soft and fair,
Not her, but thee, I love.

Stay, wild in brow, severe in mien,
Stay! and ward off the foe;
Who, unrelenting smiles serene,
Yet tells me I must go.

Forsake these hospitable halls,
Where Truth and Friendship dwell,
To these high towers and ancient walls,
Pronounce a long farewell.

Alas! will Time's rapacious hand,
These golden days restore?
Or will he suffer me to taste
These golden days no more?

Will he permit that here again,
I turn my willing feet?
That my glad eyes may here again,
The look of kindness meet?

That here I ever may behold,
Felicity to dwell,
And often have the painful task

Of sighing out farewell?

Ah, be it so! my fears I lose,
By hope's sweet visions fed;
And as I fly to seek repose,
She flutters round my bed.

NOV. 17, 1796.

TO M.I.

Thou, Margaret, lov'st the secret shade,
The murmuring brook, or tow'ring tree;
The village cot within the glade,
And lonely walk have charms for thee.

To thee more dear the jasmine bow'r,
That shelt'ring, undisturb'd retreat,
Than the high canopy of pow'r,
Or Luxury's embroider'd seat.

More sweet the early morning breeze,
Whose odours fill the rural vale,
The waving bosom of the seas,

When ruffled by the rising gale.

Than all which pride or pomp bestow,
To grace the lofty Indian maid,
Who prizes more the diamond's glow,
Than all in humbler vest array'd.

Sweet is the rural festive song,
Which sounds so wildly o'er the plain,
When thoughtless mirth the notes prolong,
And heart-felt pleasure pours the strain.

Sweet is the dance where light and gay,
The village maiden trips along;
Her simple robe in careless play,
As her fleet step winds round the throng.

Sweet is the labourer's blazing fire,
When evening shades invite to rest;
Though weary, home does joy inspire,
And social love dilates his breast.

His rural lass with glee prepares,
The dainties fondness made her hoard;
Her husband now the banquet shares,
And children croud around the board.

Ah! who could wish to view the air
Of listless ease and languid wealth?
Who with such pleasures could compare
The joys of innocence and health?

AUGUST 20, 1796.

CANTATA. DEL METASTASIO.

"D'atre nubi è il sol ravvolto,
Luce infausta il Ciel colora.
Pur chi sa? Quest' alma ancora
La speranza non perdè.

Non funesta ogni tempesta
Co' naufragj all' onde il seno;
Ogni tuono, ogni baleno
Sempre un fulmine non è."

TRANSLATION.

Dark, mournful clouds hang o'er the sun,
Lights gleam portentous in the air,
And yet who knows? This troubled heart
Still gives not up to blank despair.

Not big with shipwrecks every storm,
That sweeps the bosom of the main,
Nor does the threatening, turbid sky,
Always the thunder-bolt contain.

LA FORTUNA. DELLO STESSO.

A chi serena io miro,
Chiaro è di notte il cielo:
Torna per lui nel gelo
La terra a germogliar.

Ma se a taluno io giro
Torbido il guardo, e fosco,
Fronde gli niega il bosco,
Onde non trova in mar.

TRANSLATION.

To him whom kindly I behold,
The midnight sky is clear,
And 'mid the wintry frost and cold,
The blushing flowers appear.

But to the wretch who meets my eye,
When kindled by disdain,
The very grove will leaves deny,
And waveless be the main.

CANTATA DELLO STESSO.

Finchè un zeffiro soave
Tien del mar l'ira placata,
Ogni nave
È fortunata,
È felice ogni nocchier;

È ben prova di coraggio
Incontrar l'onde funeste,
Navigar fra le tempeste,
E non perdere il sentier.

TRANSLATION.

Whilst zephyr sooths the angry waves
Of Ocean into rest,
Each vessel is in safety borne,
And every pilot blest.

But he indeed demands our praise,
Who stems the tempest's force,
And midst the ire of hostile waves,
Pursues his destin'd course.

SONETTO.

DI GIOVANNI DELLA CASA.

Oh sonno, oh della cheta, umida, ombrosa
Notte placido figlio; oh de' mortali
Egri conforto, oblio dolce de' mali,
Sì gravi, ond' è la vita aspra, e nojosa:
Soccorri al core omai, che langue, e posa
Non have; e queste membra stanche, e frali

Solleva: a me ten vola, oh sonno, e l'ali
Tue brune sovra me distendi, e posa.
Ov' è il silenzio, che'l dì fugge, e'l lume?
E i lievi sogni, che con non secure
Vestigia di seguirti han per costume?
Lasso, che'nvan te chiamo, e queste oscure,
E gelide ombre invan lusingo; oh piume
D'asprezza colme; oh notti acerbe, e dure!

SONNET, TO SLEEP.

TRANSLATION.

Son of the silent, dark, and humid Night,
Consoler of the wretched, by whose sway
The gloomy train of ills are put to flight,
That blacken Life's uncertain, tedious day,

O! succour now this restless, pining heart!
Give to these feeble, weary limbs repose!
Fly to me, Sleep! and let thy sombre wings
Over my couch their dusky plumes disclose!

O! where is Silence, who avoids the light?

Where the wild dreams that flutter in thy train?
Alas! in vain I call thee, cruel Night!
And flatter these insensate shades in vain.

And oh! without thy cheering dews are shed,
How full of hardships is the downy bed!

EDITHA.

Breathing the violet-scented gale,
Near to a river's limpid source,
Which, through a wide-extended vale,
Wound slowly on its sleeping course,

Attended by a youthful pair,
With rubied lip and roving eye,
Oft would fair Editha repair,
And let her children wander nigh.

There pleas'd behold their footsteps turn,
To each new object in their way,
Their ringlets glittering in the sun,
Their faces careless, blythe, and gay.

Once, when they drest their flaxen hair,
With flow'rets wild of various hue,
And with a proud, exulting air,
To their delighted parent drew:

"Ah! thus may every day arise!
And pleasure thus your hearts, pervade!"
The widow'd mother fondly cries,
"Before the youthful blossoms fade.

"My sighs are all dispers'd in air,
Resign'd to fate, I weep no more,
Your welfare now is all my care,
Yet am I constant as before.

"The world, because a vermil bloom,
Tinges my yet unfading cheek,
Says I forget my William's tomb,
A new and earthly love to seek.

"Because I join the social train,
With lip that wears a kindred smile;
And a gay sonnet's lively strain,
Does oft the lonely hour beguile:

"Because no longer now I mourn,
With sweeping robes of sable hue;

No more I clasp the marble urn,
Or vainly bid the world adieu.

"Ah! ill my secret soul they know,
Where my lost hero still remains,
Where memory makes my bosom glow,
And binds me still in closer chains.

"Whoe'er hath seen my William's form,
Heighten'd with every martial grace,
The ever-varying, unknown charm,
Wich beam'd in his expressive face;

"Or heard his fine ideas try,
In Fancy's fairy garb to teach,
While the sweet language of his eye,
Excell'd the eloquence of speech,

"Could ne'er suppose my faith would fail,
Or aught again this heart enslave;
That absence would o'er love prevail,
Or hope be bounded by the grave.

"Could all but I his merit know?
His wit and talents see?
And is his name by all below
Remember'd, but by me?

"No, ne'er will I the memory lose,
Though from my sight thy form is flown,
Of tenderness for other's woes,
And noble firmness in thy own.

"No slavish fear thy soul depress,
Of Death, or his attendant train;
For in thy pure and spotless breast,
The fear of heav'n did only reign.

"Thus, when the still-unsated waves
Spread o'er thy head their whelming arms,
When horrid darkness reign'd around,
And lightnings flash'd their dire alarms,

13"When, wing'd with death, each moment flew,
And blood the foaming ocean stain'd,
Thy courage cool, consistent, true,
Its native energy maintain'd.

"And when the fatal moment came,
The bullet enter'd in thy side,
Only thy spirit's beauteous frame,
Its prisoner flying, droop'd and died.

"This is it that consoles my mind,

Which to my love aspiring flies,
And makes me hope, in future days,
To hail my William in the skies.

"Should tears from my pale eyelids steal,
I teach my children's how to flow,
And make their little bosoms feel,
Before their time, the touch, of woe.

"I will not weep! the world shall see
That I a nobler tribute pay;
More grateful both to heaven and thee,
By guiding them in virtue's way."

Embracing then her fondest cares,
She cast her raptur'd eyes above,
And breath'd to heav'n emphatic pray'rs,
Of mingled reverence and love.

APRIL 15, 1795.

13: I know not if I have expressed myself with much clearness here, but I meant to describe a sea-fight as concisely as possible.

TO M.I.

Light breezes dance along the air,
The sky in smiles is drest,
And heav'ns pure vault, serene and fair,
Pourtrays the cheerful breast.

Each object on this moving ball
Assumes a lovely hue;
So fair good-humour brightens all
That comes within her view.

Her presence glads the youthful train,
Reanimates the gay,
And, round her, by the couch of pain,
The light-wing'd graces play.

Her winning mein and prompt reply,
Can sullen pride appease;
And the sweet arching of her eye
E'en apathy must please.

To you, with whom the damsel dwells
A voluntary guest,
To you, Maria, memory tells,
This tribute is addrest.

The feeble strains that I bequeath,

With melody o'erpay;
And let thy lov'd piano breathe
A sweet responsive lay.

Although the mellow sounds will rise,
So distant from my ear,
The charmer Fancy, when she tries,
Can make them present here.

Can paint thee, as with raptur'd bend,
You hail the powers of song;
When the light fingers quick descend,
And fly the notes along:

Feel the soft chord of sadness meet,
An echo in the soul,
And waking joy the strains repeat,
When Mirth's-quick measures roll.

This "mistress of the powerful spell,"
Can every joy impart;
And ah! you doubtless know too well
How she can wring the heart.

She rules me with despotic reign,
As now I say *adieu;*
And makes me feel a sort of pain,

As if I spoke to you.

FEB. 14, 1797.

WRITTEN IN

ZIMMERMANN'S SOLITUDE.

Hail, melancholy sage! whose thoughtful eye,
Shrunk from the mere *spectator's* careless gaze,
And, in retirement sought the social smile,
The heart-endearing aspect, and the voice
Of soothing tenderness, which Friendship breathes,
And which sounds far more grateful to the ear,
Than the soft notes of distant flute at eve,
Stealing across the waters: Zimmermann!
Thou draw'st not Solitude as others do,
With folded arms, with pensive, nun-like air,
And tearful eye, averted from mankind.
No! warm, benign, and cheerful, she appears
The friend of Health, of Piety, and Peace;
The kind Samaritan that heals our woes,
The nurse of Science, and, of future fame
The gentle harbinger: her meek abode
Is that dear home, which still the virtuous heart,
E'en in the witching maze of Pleasure's dance,
In wild Ambition's dream, regards with love,
And hopes, with fond security, to pass
The evening of a long-protracted day,
Serenely joyful, there.

IN MEMORY OF

MR. AGOSTINO ISOLA,

OF CAMBRIDGE,

Who died on the 5th of June, 1797.

Awake, O Gratitude! nor let the tears
Of selfish Sorrow smother up thy voice,
When it should speak of a departed friend.
A tender friend, the first I ever lost!
For Destiny till now was merciful,
And though I oft have felt a transient pang,
For worth unknown, and wept awhile for those,
Whom long acquaintance only made me love,
No keen regret laid pining at my heart,
Nor Memory in the solitary hour,
Would sting with grief, as when she speaks
Thy virtue, knowledge, wisdom, gentleness,
Thy venerable age, and says that I
Had once the happiness to call thee friend.

Yes! I once bore that title, and my heart
Thought nobler of itself, that one so good,
So honor'd, so rever'd, should give it me.
O *Isola!* when that glad season comes,
Which brought redemption to a ruin'd world,
And, like thee, hides beneath the snow of age,
A gay, benevolent, and feeling heart,
I hop'd again to hear thy tongue repeat,
With youthful warmth and zealous energy,
Those passages, where Poetry assumes
An air divine, and wakes th' attentive soul
To holy rapture! Then you promis'd me
The luxury to weep o'er Dante's muse,

And fair Italia's loftier poets hail.

I have often heard

That years would blunt the feelings of the soul,

And apathy ice the once-glowing heart.

Injurious prejudice! Dear, guileless friend!

Thou read'st mankind, but saw not, or forgot

Their faults and vices; for thy breast was still

The residence of sweet Simplicity,

Daughter of letter'd Wisdom, and the friend

Of Love and Pity. Happy soul, farewell!

Long shall we mourn thee! longer will it be,

"Ere we shall look upon thy like again!"

This humble tribute to the memory of my venerated friend, was written in the first impulse of my sorrow for his loss, and though unworthy of his virtues, is still a small memorial of my respect for a man, on whose tomb might justly be inscribed, as I have seen on an old monument:

"Heven hath his soule.

He fruits of Pietie,

This Towne his want.

Our hearts his Memorie."

TO THE NUNS OF BODNEY.

Ye holy women, say! will ye accept
The passing tribute of a humble friend?
Stranger indeed to you and to your faith,
But O! I hope not stranger to the zeal,
Which warm'd your bosoms in Religion's cause.
When impious men commanded you to break
The vow which bound your souls, and which in youth
Warm Piety's emphatic lips had made.
Say! will ye suffer me on that rude tomb,
Where she reposes (whose benignant smile,
Whose animated, life-inspiring eye,
And faded form, majestic, still appears
In Thought's delusive hour) to shed a tear?
On her, whose sainted look, though seen but once,
I never can forget, till Time shall wrap
The veil of Death around me, and make dumb
The voice of Memory. Ah! "how low she lies!"
No marble monument to speak her praise,
And tell the world that here a DILLON rests.
One, who in beauty's prime forsook the world,
And, *self-bereav'd* of all it holds most dear,
Retir'd, to pass the pilgrimage of life,
In solemn prayer and peaceful solitude.
Ah, vain desire! Ambition's scowling eye
Must see the cloister, as the palace, low,
And meek-ey'd Quiet quit her last abode,
Ere he can pause to look upon the wreck,
And rue the wild impatience of his hand.

Hail! blessed spirit! This rude cypher'd stone.
On which a sister's pensive eye shall muse
In sorrow, and another relative
In sweet, though mournful, recollection, bend,

Shall call a tear into the stranger's eye
Whene'er he hears the tale, yet make him proud
That Britain's hospitable land should yield
All that you could accept, *an humble grave.*

Written in London, on the 19th of March, 1796.

A lov'd companion, chosen friend,
Does at this hour depart,
Whom the dear name of father binds
Still closer to my heart.

On him may joy-dispensing heav'n
Each calm delight bestow,
And eas'd of peace-destroying care
His life serenely flow!

Did I but know his bosom calm,
And free from anxious fear,
Around me in more cheerful hues
Would every scene appear.

And I will hope that he, who ne'er
Repin'd at heav'n's decree,
But ever patient and resign'd,
Submissive bent the knee:

Who, best of fathers, never sought
For arbitrary sway,
But free within each youthful mind,
Bade Reason lead the way.

Who taught us, 'stead of servile fear,
A warm esteem to prove,
And bade each act of duty spring,
From gratitude and love.

Yes, I must hope that generous mind
With many cares opprest,
Shall in the winter of his days
With sweet repose be blest.

A friend, a year or two ago, gave me Joseph's Reconciliation with his Brethren, *as a subject to write upon; but I was afraid of not treating it in such a manner as a sacred story deserved, and gave up the attempt, when I had written little more than the following lines, to account for their not knowing him, although he well remembered them; and am persuaded to let them appear here.*

FRAGMENT.

They, ere he left them, had attain'd their prime
And were less alter'd by the hand of Time;
But, the slim youth no longer met their view,

Fair, as the fancy e'er a seraph drew.
Who still, upborne by joy, in smiles was found,
With step elate that scarcely press'd the ground.
Before a grief had raz'd his youthful breast,
Or care had robb'd his brilliant eyes of rest.
When lofty visions swam before his sight,
And dreams of empire wrapt his soul at night.
Whose hair luxuriant flow'd in glossy pride,
And, from his snowy forehead, wav'd aside;
Which, vein'd with purest azure, rose serene,
And threw complacence o'er a rapturous mien.
The wandering light that sparkled in his eye,
The rounding lip of liveliest crimson dye,
The speaking form, by each emotion sway'd,
The voice, that softest music had convey'd,
Were now matur'd. No more the child they saw,
But one, with majesty, inspiring awe;
Whose silken locks no more in ringlets flow,
But gold and purple bind his manly brow:
No more the envied robe his limbs invest,
In all the pomp of eastern monarchs drest.
The sun of Egypt had embrown'd his face,
And time had ripen'd every youthful grace.

As when the morn, in vivid colours gay,
And tender beauty, flies to meet the day,
Her lively tints lose their primeval hue,
The white and saffron mingle with the blue,
A glowing blush o'er the whole ether reigns,
But not a cloud its genuine tint retains.

FRAGMENT.

Where yonder mossy ruins lie,
And desolation strikes the eye,
A noble mansion, high and fair,
Once rear'd its turrets in the air.
There infant warriors drew their breath,
And learn'd to scorn the fear of death.
In halls where martial trophies hung,
They listen'd while the minstrels sung,
Of pain and glory, toil and care,
And all the horrid charms of war:
There caught the fond desire of fame,
And panted for a hero's name.
Alas! too oft in youthful bloom,
Renown has crown'd the early tomb,
Has pierc'd the widow's bosom deep,
And taught the mother's eyes to weep.
She, on whose tale the stripling hung,
While pride and sorrow rul'd her tongue.
His father's gallant acts to tell,
How bold he fought, how bravely fell.

Methinks e'en now I hear her speak,
I see the tear upon her cheek;
The musing boy's abstracted brow,
And the high-arching eye below.
The stifled sigh and anxious heave,
The kindling heart which dares not grieve;
The finely-elevated head,
The hand upon the bosom spread,
Proclaim him wrought by potent charms,
And speak his very soul in arms.

Incautious zeal! what hast thou done?
The tale has robb'd thee of thy son.
And while thy pious tears deplore,

The loss of him who lives no more,
Ambition wakes her restless fire,
The boy will emulate his sire,

Written April the 18th, 1796

The beauteous queen of social love,
Descending from the realms above,
Through the wide space of ether flew,
With care this little world to view,
Till, tir'd with wandering, at the last,
Through every different climate past,
She sought not out a splendid dome,
But made this humble cot her home.

The sweetest lyre would strive in vain,
To sing the pleasures of her reign,
Whose powerful influence does impart,
New softness to the feeling heart,
Bids it each narrow thought resign,
And fills it with a warmth benign.

From morning till the close of day,
Here all a grateful homage pay,
For here she plays her harmless wiles,
And scatters her endearing smiles;
Here no proud rivals intervene,
And all, though glowing, is serene.
Here, since she first her visit paid,
Still has the sweet enchantress staid,
And never met a single slight,
Or spread her snowy plumes for flight.

Contented 'neath the humble roof;
No timid heart is kept aloof;
A kind and condescending guest,
She lightens each despairing breast;
Where pain her poignant venom spreads,

The balm of tenderness she sheds,
Which breathes a calm repose around,
And heals at last the burning wound.

When the heart throbs with bitter woe,
Her winning mien disarms the foe,
And the kind glances of her eye,
Force the desponding power to fly.
She gives a zest to every joy,
Forbids tranquillity to cloy,
Softens misfortune, chases fear,
And balm distills in every tear.
'Tis she alone can make us know,
A truly blissful hour below,
Can smooth the furrow'd brow of life,
And hush the thundering voice of strife.

O, may she still exert her power,
Still lead us to the rural bower,
Which vaunting Pride does ne'er disgrace,
Or critic Envy's spiteful face.
Here Raymond ever shall delight,
To sit and watch the closing night;
And open-hearted Gertrude here,
With her sweet infant shall appear.
Here oft her brother shall prepare,
A wreath for Mary's curling hair;
While soft-voic'd Anna, fond of play,
And all the train, alert and gay,
In healthful games shall frolic round,
And revel on the mossy ground.

Here Edmund shall forget his care,
And often fill an elbow chair;
While Sophia, friendly and sincere,
Shall ever find a welcome here.

Yet would my hovering fancy trace,
The features of each happy face;
And sympathy informs my mind,
That they the same emotions find;
That in each scene of harmless glee,
Memory recalls the absent three:
And all, though distance strives to part,
Will hold communion in the heart.

FINIS.